KW-481-175

50000000039044

ANIMAL POEMS & RHYMES

CHOSEN BY
GRACE JONES

ILLUSTRATED BY
DRUE RINTOUL

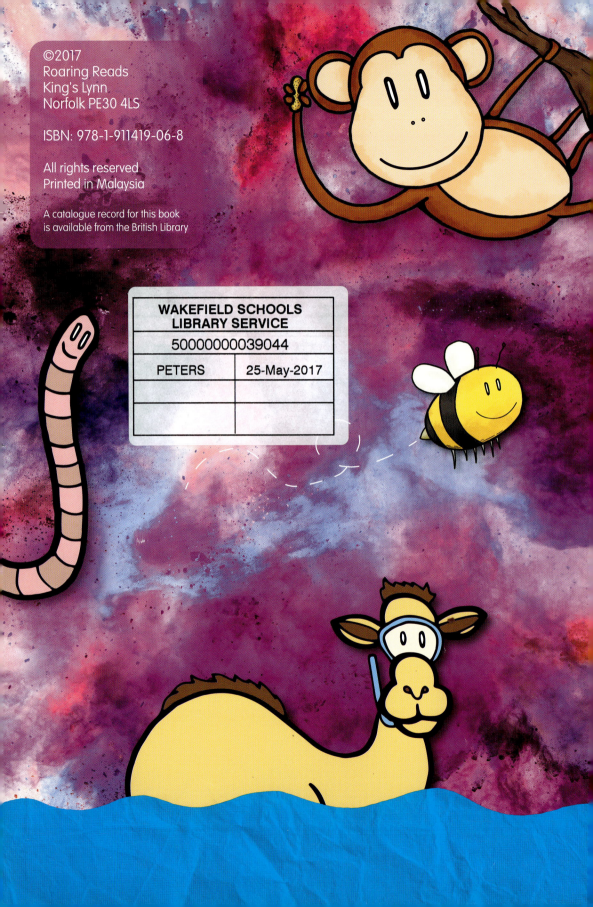

©2017
Roaring Reads
King's Lynn
Norfolk PE30 4LS

ISBN: 978-1-911419-06-8

A catalogue record for this book
is available from the British Library

All rights reserved
Printed in Malaysia

WAKEFIELD SCHOOLS LIBRARY SERVICE	
50000000039044	
PETERS	25-May-2017

CONTENTS

HELLO WORLD

The world's a big, round ball that's sometimes scary,
with animals that are big, small and sometimes hairy.
Let's explore this planet and see what we find,
I'm sure we'll find creatures of every kind.

SPLISH SPLASH WHALE

Splish, splash and off she goes,
a wailing whale in the night.
Splish, splash and off she goes,
swimming, sailing, singing loudly.

Splish, splash, she breaks the water,
jumping high above the waves.
Splish, splash, she breaks the water,
blowhole bobbing below the birds.

Splish, splash and down she dives,
shooting, spraying, spouting water.
Splish, splash and down she dives,
deeper down into the dark.

Charlie Ogden

MEET THE ANIMALS

I went to the garden to see what I could see,

I found a hungry caterpillar staring back at me,

a little chirping blackbird high up in a tree,

and a busy, buzzing bee.

I dived into the sea to see what lived under me,

I found a fish hiding in a seaweed tree,

an octopus having afternoon tea,

and a mermaid who waved at me.

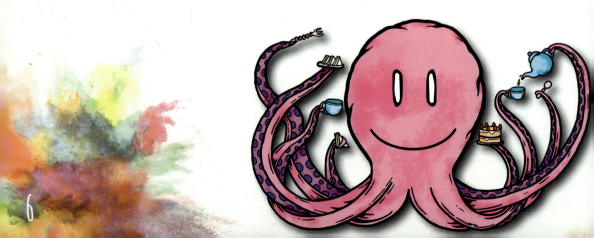

I walked through the jungle to see what I could see,
I found an enormous elephant chasing a tiny bee,
a mischievous monkey throwing nuts at me,
and a slithering snake snaking down from a tree.

I came to meet the monsters who lived up in the air,
I met a monster who had wriggling worms for hair,
one with five eyes who had trumpets for ears,
and a huge, scary one sleeping in his lair ...
enter if you dare!

Grace Jones

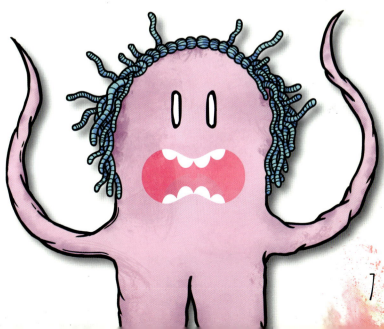

LITTLE LOST BEAR

"Have you seen my family, little mouse?"
"No Baby Bear," he said in a hurry
and back in his house, he ran in a scurry.

"Have you seen my family, little hedgehog?"
"Yes Baby Bear," he said with a smile,
"They went that way, they've been there for a while".

As Baby Bear ran towards his family,
he cried "I've been very scared,
I've seen rabbits and mice but no brown bears!"

"I'm hungry now mum, can we go home for tea?",
"Yes, Baby Bear. Is there a cuddle for me?".

Kayleigh Briggs

THE GREEDY QUEEN BEE

The most greedy and wicked queen

is not one you would like to meet.

She's spoilt rotten and mean,

not one you should ever greet!

She only eats yummy honey,

for breakfast, lunch and tea.

She likes it yellow, sticky and runny,

and slurps it all up with glee!

Whatever you hear or see,

she'll give you a nasty sting.

So never upset a queen bee,

because she's a nasty, wicked thing!

Steffi Cavell-Clarke

GARTH
THE GIRAFFE

Meet Garth the giraffe.
He's a bit of a wreck,
because everyone laughs
at the size of his neck.

Garth was made so sad
when they called him weird,
that he went out and grabbed
a fake, bushy beard.

He hated his throat
so he spent ten dollars,
buying a new coat
with a ten-foot collar.

But now Garth the giraffe
wears his new giraffe-scarf,
and today there aren't half
the number of laughs.

Charlie Ogden

TRINA THE BALLERINA

Have you ever seen Trina?
The one in the ballet shoes?
She's a famous ballerina,
with a huge collection of tutus.

Trina shines and sparkles,
as she twirls and swirls.
She even wiggles and wobbles,
more than the other girls!

Trina can jump and prance,
she's very light on her feet.
If you ever see her dance,
you'll be in for a lovely treat.

So if you love ballet,
she's a great entertainer.
But if she comes your way
you may end up in danger!

Steffi Cavell-Clarke

COUNTING CREATURES

1 One Orange Octopus

2 Two Tiny Turtles

3 Three Talking Turkeys

4 Four Furry Foxes

5 Five Friendly Frogs

6 Six Sleeping Sheep

7 Seven Sneaky Squirrels

8 Eight Enormous Elephants

9 Nine Naughty Newts

10 Ten Terrifying Tigers

Kayleigh Briggs

THE TECHNICOLOURED DREAMGOAT

If you've ever met a goat who's not quite as they seem,
you might think they're a ghost or maybe just a dream.

But there once was a goat with a very special coat,
he was yellow, blue and green with many colours in-between.

He loved to dance and show off his groovy moves,
but he never got the chance to shake his disco hooves.

So the next time that you dream of magical coats,
remember to believe in technicoloured dreamgoats.

Grace Jones

THE WORM

I'm a wriggly worm,

I like to wiggle and squirm.

I can be found,

down in the ground.

I love to get stuck,

in all of the dirt and muck.

Because I'm a wriggly worm,

and I like to wiggle and squirm.

Steffi Cavell-Clarke

I'VE SEEN A MOOSE BAKE BANANA BREAD ...

People say fish have fins and scales,

people say birds are smaller than whales,

people say wolves have hairy tails,

people say goats are bigger than snails.

But they might be wrong, they can tell lies.

I've seen animals with my own eyes,

that prove that otters live in the skies,

and that pandas make excellent pies.

I've met a bat with a big, pink trunk.

I've seen a wombat box with a skunk.

I've met a cat who could speak Greek.

I've seen a rat pick food from its beak.

I've met a goose with horns on its head.

I've seen a moose bake banana bread.

I've seen a camel swim in a stream.

Oh, wait a minute, that was a dream!

Charlie Ogden

CROCODILE SMILE

A crocodile's smile is a wonder and a treat.

Never have you seen this many teeth so white and neat.

But be careful if you meet a happy croc out in the street,

as a smiling crocodile just sees you as a piece of meat!

Every creature knows the crocodile's smile is a trap.

Any fish could tell you that he's not a happy chap.

The birds never go near him, not even when he naps,

because those jaws could close around them with a snap!

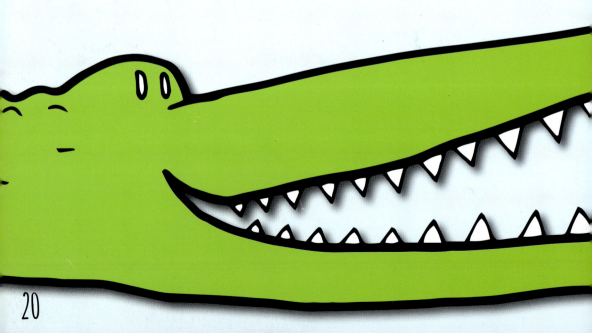

The crocodile's smile is brightest when he sees his lunch,
a tasty flock of flamingos stood in the tightest bunch.
He knows that these flamingos cannot kick or punch,
so he puts them in his mouth and eats them with a crunch!

A smiling crocodile means that you should run and dash,
as a croc's idea of fun is to squish and thrash.
Paying him won't work, he won't accept fish or cash.
He'll just eat you too - then swim away - splish splash!

Charlie Ogden

THE LONDON ZOO

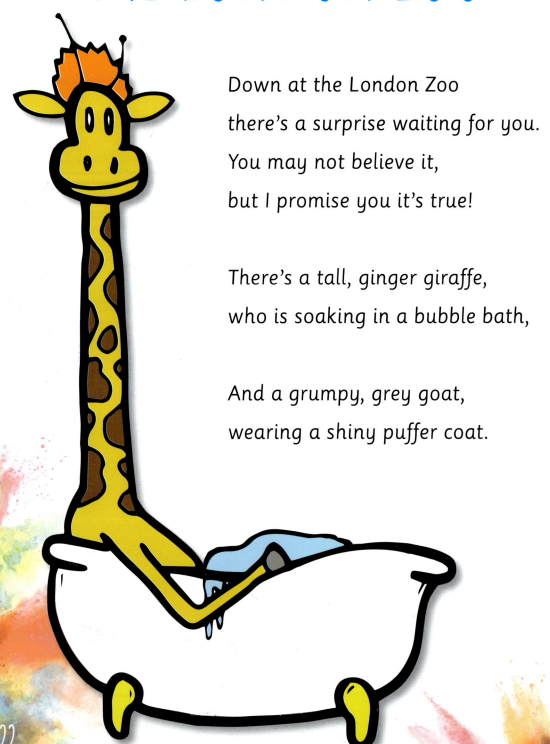

Down at the London Zoo
there's a surprise waiting for you.
You may not believe it,
but I promise you it's true!

There's a tall, ginger giraffe,
who is soaking in a bubble bath,

And a grumpy, grey goat,
wearing a shiny puffer coat.

There's an elephant with a hat on his head,
who's jumping on his big, bouncy bed,

While the Egyptian crocodile,
tries out a new style.

And don't forget the bear,
carefully brushing her hair.

Down at the London Zoo
there's a surprise waiting for you.
You may not believe it,
but I promise you it's true!

Steffi Cavell-Clarke

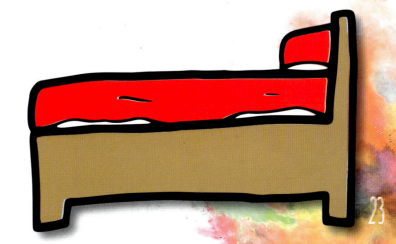

GOODBYE WORLD

Now you know for yourself how big this world is,
and how many animals sneak up on small kids.
But you shouldn't be scared, little boys and girls,
just take care of the animals and take care of the world.